PINGU

Celebrates Christmas

BBC CHILDREN'S BOOKS

It was Christmas at the South Pole. In Pingu's house everyone was very excited. Pingu rushed to open the final window in his advent calendar.

"Christmas has come at last," he told his baby sister, Pinga.

"Whoopee!" shouted Pinga, and jumped up and down.

Mum was busy making special Christmas biscuits. First, she rolled out the biscuit dough.

"Can we help?" asked Pingu and Pinga, pushing their flippers into the sticky mixture.

"Don't touch," said Mum crossly. "You can go and lick out the mixing bowl instead."

Pingu and Pinga dipped their flippers into the biscuit mixture. It tasted delicious and they gobbled away greedily. It was also lovely and messy.

Next Mum cut out the biscuit shapes and put them on the baking tray. There were stars and moons.

Then Mum let Pingu paint the shapes with a special brush.

"I want a go, too," whined Pinga.

"Too bad!" said Pingu and painted a bright yellow stripe on Pinga's face.

In no time at all the biscuits were ready.

"Ow!" said Mum as she opened the hot oven door and took out the baking tray. She put the cooked biscuits down on the table quickly.

Pingu and Pinga couldn't wait
to try the biscuits, but Mum
stopped them just in time.
   "Get your flippers off,"
she snapped. "The biscuits
are for later."

At that moment Dad came home carrying an exciting-looking present wrapped in green paper. Pingu and Pinga charged up to him.

"Dad, Dad! Can we open it now?" they both shouted together.

"No," said Dad firmly. "We'll all open our presents later."

And he placed the present high up out of Pingu's and Pinga's reach.

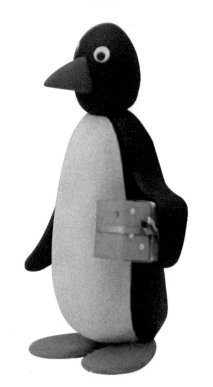

Then Dad saw the biscuits.

"Mmmm," he said. "Just what I need after a hard morning's work at the Post Office."

Mum slapped Dad's flipper as he reached out for a biscuit. "No you don't!" she said. "I've got a lot to do now, so why don't you all go off and buy a Christmas tree."

"Good idea," said Dad. And
taking Pingu and Pinga with him,
he drove off to the Christmas tree
market in the post truck.

There were lots of different trees to choose from.
"I'd like a nice tall one," said Pinga, gazing up at
the branches of the largest tree she could find.

"Don't be silly," said Pingu. "That's much too big. I bet Dad will choose a tiny one like that miserable little one over there." He pointed to the smallest tree he could see.

"How about this one?" said Dad, picking out a lovely bushy tree that was just the right size.

Pinga paid for the tree while Dad loaded it onto the post truck.

"Happy Christmas," Pingu called out to the Christmas tree seller as they set off for home.

"A Happy Christmas to you, too," the penguin shouted back and waved cheerfully.

Back at home Pingu and Pinga went running in to tell Mum about the tree.

"Come and look," they shouted.

Mum came bustling out carrying an armful of presents and a huge box of Christmas decorations.

Mum's arms were so full that she couldn't see
where she was putting her flippers and – whoops –
she tripped right over a piece of rope that was lying
on the ground. The parcels all went flying.

"How can you be so clumsy?" shouted Dad. "Now you've gone and dropped all the Christmas decorations."

"Well, if you hadn't left the rope there in the first place, I would never have tripped over at all!" Mum shouted back crossly.

Soon Mum and Dad were having a big argument. Their voices grew louder and louder.

Suddenly they noticed Pingu and Pinga watching them, looking very upset.

"It's Christmas," sniffed Pingu miserably. "Please be friends with each other."

"Mum, Dad," sobbed Pinga. "I don't like it when you fight."

Mum and Dad looked at each other and realised how silly they were being.

"Will you make it up?" said Dad.

"Of course," said Mum, smiling.

So they kissed and rubbed beaks and then burst out laughing.

Pingu and Pinga were delighted to see that Mum and Dad were friends again.

Now it was time to decorate the tree. Mum and Dad wanted to do it secretly so Pingu and Pinga were sent indoors.

"No peeping!" Mum said as she locked the door and blocked up the keyhole with a lump of snow.

21

Inside the house Pingu put on a record of
Christmas music and then he and Pinga decided to
wrap up their presents.

Pinga tied some bright gold ribbon and a bow on her present to Dad. Pingu had fun sticking glittery stars on his present to Mum.

Outside the house Mum and Dad added the finishing touches to the tree.

"It looks beautiful," sighed Mum.

"It's the best tree we've ever had," said Dad.

At last Mum came to unlock the door of the house. Pingu and Pinga were led out into the snow and there they saw the tree sparkling with shiny baubles, bows and tinsel.

"It's wonderful!" they gasped.

Then they started opening their presents. Mum unwrapped her present from Pingu.

"A muff!" she exclaimed. "Now I'll be able to keep my flippers lovely and warm."

Dad was very pleased with his spotty bow tie from Pinga. "I shall look the smartest penguin in the South Pole," he said as he tried it on.

27

Pingu was very lucky with his presents. The first one he opened was a colouring book. Then he unwrapped a big stripy ball.

"Look at me!" he shouted as he spun it round on his flipper.

His last present was a pair of ear muffs. "They're just what I wanted," he said.

Pinga opened some lovely presents, too. Grandpa had sent her a teddy bear. Pinga threw her arms round it and kissed it.

Her present from Mum and Dad was a new dummy. And Pingu gave her a warm, woolly scarf.

When everyone had opened their presents, Dad announced that it was time to sing some carols. So as the stars sparkled in the sky, and the Christmas bells rang out in the snowy evening air, the whole family stood by the Christmas tree and sang together.

HAPPY CHRISTMAS!

Published by BBC Children's Books
a division of BBC Enterprises Limited
Woodlands, 80 Wood Lane, London W12 0TT
First published 1994
Text © 1994 BBC Children's Books
Stills © 1994 Editoy/SRG/BBC Enterprises
Design © 1994 BBC Children's Books
Pingu © 1994 Editoy/SRG/BBC Enterprises

ISBN 0 563 40352 7

Typeset by BBC Children's Books
Colour separations by DOT Gradations, Chelmsford
Printed and bound by Cambus Litho, East Kilbride